Fimble Valley

ide

Bedroom
and Bathroom

Living Room

Home

BBC CHILDREN'S BOOKS
Published by the Penguin Group
Penguin Books Ltd, 80 Strand, London WC2R 0RL, England
Penguin Putnam Inc., 375 Hudson Street, New York, New York 10014, USA
Penguin Books Australia Ltd, 250 Camberwell Road, Camberwell, Victoria 3124, Australia
Canada, India, New Zealand, South Africa
Published by BBC Children's Books, 2005
Text and design © BBC Children's Books, 2005
10 9 8 7 6 5 4 3 2
Written by Susie Day. Based on the television series script written by
Lucinda Whiteley and Mike Watts and a short story by Christine Secombe.
"The Roly Mo Show" © Novel Finders Limited 2004. All rights reserved
Roly Mo and Rockit ™ BBC. Yugo, Migo and Little Bo ™ Novel
Finders Limited
BBC and logo © and ™ BBC 1996
CBeebies and logo ™ BBC. © BBC 2002
All rights reserved
ISBN 1 405 90040 7
Printed in Italy

Growing Up

Little Bo hung up her rucksack on its usual peg. She noticed how easy the peg was for her to reach.

"It must be because I'm getting bigger," she thought. "After all, it is nearly time for my birthday!"

She felt sure Roly Mo would notice how grown-up she was now.

"Hello there, Little Bo," said Roly Mo. Little Bo stood up as straight as she possibly could.

"I see you're looking very tall today," said Roly.

"I'm growing up," said Little Bo proudly.
"So you are," said Roly. "Do you
think you're grown-up enough to
choose today's story?"

"Books over here,
books over there,
find me a book with a
story to share."

"Please may I have
a special story,
just for me," said
Little Bo.

When I Was One

It was the day before Josh's birthday. He was so excited, he couldn't talk about anything else.

"What was I like when I was one?" he asked, at breakfast.

"When you were one, you'd only just begun," said Mum. "Just like Martha."

Baby Martha was smearing jam on her face with one hand and tipping juice over the table with the other. Josh was sure he had never been so messy.

"And when I was two?" he asked, in the garden.

"You found plenty to do," said Mum. "You used to play in the mud."

The mud looked black and sticky. Josh was sure he had never wanted to play there.

"And when I was three?" he asked later.

"There was lots to see," said Mum. "You painted pictures, like this one."

Josh thought the picture was quite good.

"What will I be like when I'm five?" he asked, at bedtime.

"Wait until tomorrow," said Mum. "Then we'll find out!"

The End

"Baby Mo is my little sister, just like Martha is Josh's," said Little Bo, looking at the photograph of her family on the wall.

"So she is," said Roly.

"And it's nearly my birthday, just like it was nearly Josh's," said Little Bo. "I'm getting bigger all the time!"

She dashed off to tell Yugo and Migo how grown-up she was.

"Yugo! Migo!" called Little Bo. "Where are you?"

But Yugo and Migo were too busy to talk.

"Can't stop, Little Bo!" said Yugo.

"Lots to do today!" said Migo.

"Like bouncing!"
"And snootling!"
"And hiding!"
The Snoots disappeared.
"But...but I wanted to..." said Little Bo, getting cross. "Oh, never mind."

"Yugo and Migo are just babies, Uncle Roly," said Little Bo. "From now on I'm going to do grown-up things with you. Like mending things, and reading the Daily Mole, and..."

"Listening to the radio?" said Roly. "You're just in time for my favourite gardening programme."

Little Bo sat on the sofa, feeling excited. Listening to the radio seemed a very grown-up thing to do.

She watched Roly carefully, to make sure she was doing it right. When Roly nodded, she nodded. When Roly chuckled, she chuckled. When Roly fell asleep, she closed her eyes and pretended to snore.

"Toot toot!"
Yugo and Migo popped
up beside Little Bo.
   "Shhh!" she whispered.
"I'm listening to the radio
with Uncle Roly."
   "The radio?" said Migo.
   "Ooooeee!" said Yugo.
   Little Bo began to giggle.
   Roly started to wake up.
   Pop! Pop! The snoots
disappeared behind
the sofa.

"Would you like to do something else grown-up now, Bo?" said Roly.

"Squeak!" squeaked Migo, behind the sofa.

"I wonder where the Snoots have got to?" said Roly, with a twinkle in his eye.

"Honk!" honked Yugo.
Then Little Bo heard a loud "Parp!"
"Uncle Roly, that was you!"
she said.

"Yes, that was me!" said Roly.

"But you're grown-up," said Little Bo.

"That doesn't mean I can't make funny noises," said Roly. "Toot toot!"

"Squeak!" squeaked Yugo.

"Honk!" honked Migo.

"Parp!" added Little Bo. "What a Roly Moly day! It doesn't matter if I'm big or small really, does it? I can still have lots of fun!"

The End

Entrance Hall

Library

Kitchen

Roly M